This book belongs to

Bluebell Glade

Dandelion Dell

Heart of Misty Wood

Hawthorn Hedgerows

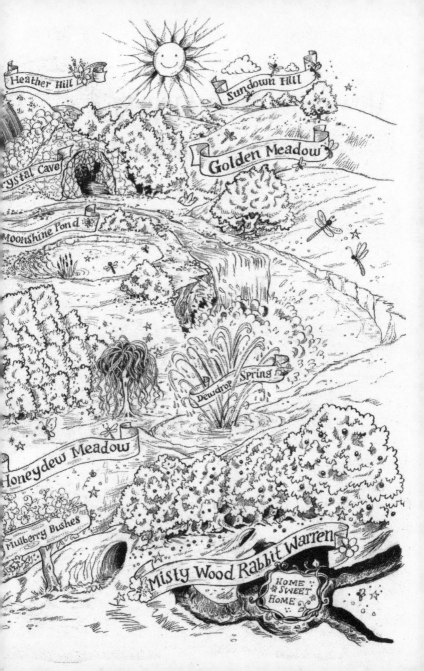

How many Fairy Animals books have you collected?

 Chloe the Kitten

 Bella the Bunny

 Paddy the Puppy

 Mia the Mouse

And there are lots more magical adventures coming very soon!

Fairy Animals

of Misty Wood

Mia the Mouse

Lily Small

EGMONT

With Special thanks to Thea Bennett

EGMONT
We bring stories to life

Mia the Mouse first published in Great Britain 2013
by Egmont UK Limited
The Yellow Building, 1 Nicholas Road, London W11 4AN

Text copyright © 2013 Hothouse Fiction Ltd
Illustrations copyright © 2013 Artful Doodlers Ltd
All rights reserved

ISBN 978 1 4052 6659 8
3 5 7 9 10 8 6 4 2

www.egmont.co.uk

www.hothousefiction.com

www.fairyanimals.com

A CIP catalogue record for this title is available from the British Library

Printed and bound in Great Britain by The CPI Group

54738/3

MIX
Paper
FSC   FSC® C018306

EGMONT LUCKY COIN

Our story began over a century ago, when seventeen-year-old Egmont Harald Petersen found a coin in the street.

He was on his way to buy a flyswatter, a small hand-operated printing machine that he then set up in his tiny apartment.

The coin brought him such good luck that today Egmont has offices in over 30 countries around the world. And that lucky coin is still kept at the company's head offices in Denmark.

 # Contents

CHAPTER ONE

A Good Little Mouse

Deep in the Heart of Misty Wood there was an oak tree so tall its branches seemed to touch the sky. Its leaves were as green as emeralds and loved to dance in

the breeze. The oak tree's thick, knobbly roots stretched deep into the soil and held the tree steady.

If you looked carefully, in between the tree roots, behind a cluster of tall green ferns, you would see a hole leading down to a cosy burrow. And if you looked very carefully indeed, you would see a little mouse sitting on the grass next to the hole. The mouse's name was Mia, and she lived in

the burrow with her mum and dad,
her grandma and her four baby
brothers and sisters.

Mia was a Moss Mouse
– one of the Fairy Animals of
Misty Wood. Her beautiful fairy
wings were transparent, just

like a dragonfly's, and when
the sunshine touched them they
twinkled violet and green. Her fur
was as golden as honey, except
on her tummy where it was snow
white, and she had long, silky
whiskers that wiggled and twirled
whenever she was excited.

Mia was making a cushion
from a ball of soft green moss.

'Pat-a-cake, pat-a-cake, pat-
a-cake!' she sang to herself as she

rolled the moss along the ground and patted it into a nice round shape with her tiny pink paws.

Just like all the Fairy Animals of Misty Wood, the Moss Mice had a special job to do, to make the wood a wonderful place to live. The mice made soft, squishy cushions out of moss and placed them all around the wood, so the other Fairy Animals would have somewhere comfortable to sit.

5

MIA THE MOUSE

'Pat, pat, pat!' Mia sang as she shaped the cushion.

'Hello, Mia!' a voice called.

There was a scrabbling noise from inside the hole, and a face with bright beady eyes and long, silvery whiskers popped out. It was Mia's dad.

'I'm afraid Grandma's come down with a nasty case of the sniffles,' he said. 'Will you go and keep her company? Mum's busy

with the babies, and I've got to go
out and collect some more moss
for our cushions.'

'Of course I will,' Mia said.

Mia's dad gave her a twinkly-
eyed smile. 'You *are* a good little
mouse! Perhaps you could tell
Grandma one of your stories. I
bet she would like that.' And with
that, he jumped out of the hole,
twirled his whiskers and unfurled
his wings. They glinted silver in the

sun. 'See you at tea time!' Mia's dad called as he flew off through the trees. He carried a big bag made from spider silk in his front paws.

Mia picked up her cushion and hurried underground. The passageway to the burrow was nice and cool and smelled of fresh earth. Mia's whiskers began to twitch. Telling stories was her favourite thing in the whole wide world. She loved it even more

than making cushions.

Mia scampered into the burrow. At one end, her mum was busy feeding the babies. At the other, Grandma was tucked up in her bed of soft moss.

Mia hopped over to her. Grandma was curled up in the middle of the bed with her nose peeping over the edge. Normally, Grandma's nose was pale pink, but today it was red. Mia went a

little closer. Normally, Grandma's
black eyes shone and there was a
happy smile on her face, but today
her eyes were bleary and she
looked sad.

'A-a-a-a-CHOO!' Grandma sneezed when she saw Mia.

'Bless you!' said Mia. She hopped on to a cushion and leaned her front paws on the edge of the bed. 'Dad said you weren't feeling well, so I've come to keep you company.'

'Ah, thank you, Mia,' replied Grandma, wiping her nose on a white daisy petal. Then she sneezed again. 'A-a-a-CHOO!'

'Oh, dear. You must be feeling

very poorly,' Mia said.

'Yes, I am.' Grandma sighed.

'My poor nose is so sore . . .

a-a-a-CHOO!'

Mia put her head to one side.

13

'Would you like me to tell you a story?'

Grandma's eyes lit up. 'Ooh, yes please! I do love your stor– a-a-a-CHOO!'

Mia sat down on the cushion she'd just made. If she could think of a really good story, Grandma might forget about her sneezes and her sore nose.

Mia's whiskers wiggled with excitement as the beginning of a

story began to form in her mind:

'Once upon a time . . . there was a caterpillar!' she started.

'A caterpillar? Well, I never,' said Grandma, with a loud sniff.

'And she was called Clarissa!' said Mia.

'That's a big name for a little caterpillar,' said Grandma.

'Oh, but she wasn't little!' cried Mia, and her whiskers twitched and wiggled so much

she had to jump down and run
round Grandma's bed. 'She was
the biggest caterpillar you've ever
seen! She was bigger than you and
me and Mum and Dad and all the
babies put together!'

'Goodness,' said Grandma.
Then she smiled. She hadn't
sneezed for quite a while now.
'How did she get to be so big?'

'Well . . .' began Mia, jumping
back on to the cushion, 'Clarissa

was very greedy. She ate and ate,

all day long.'

Grandma frowned. 'Wherever did she get all that food from?'

Mia's whiskers quivered as she thought up the answer. 'Clarissa had a best friend. His name was Archie, and he was a tiny ant. Archie brought Clarissa lots of snacks. He brought her leaves and berries and nuts and . . .'

'Lucky Clarissa!' said Grandma, wriggling upright. She looked much happier now.

Mia sat up on her hind legs on the cushion as the next part of the story came into her head. 'But one day – and this is the really scary bit of the story, Grandma – Clarissa disappeared!'

'Oh, dear!' said Grandma. 'Where had she gone?'

Mia sighed. 'Nobody knew. Archie searched all through Misty Wood but he couldn't find her anywhere.'

Grandma shook her head and her whiskers began to droop. 'That's a very sad story.'

Mia was just about to explain that she hadn't finished yet when her mum came scampering over.

'Thank you for looking after Grandma, Mia,' she said. 'The babies are asleep now, so I'll take over from you.'

Mia sighed. She was just getting to the most exciting part.

'It's all right, Mum, *I'm* looking after Grandma,' she said.

Mia's mum smiled. Then she stroked the moss cushion that Mia had just made. 'What a lovely soft cushion. Well done, Mia. There's just one thing . . .'

'Oh, Mum, I'm in the middle of telling Grandma a story!' Mia interrupted.

'I know,' Mia's mum said. 'But I just need you to fetch

something for me.'

Mia sighed. She wanted to go on with her story. She wanted to give it the best, most exciting ending ever, so that Grandma would forget all about being ill.

'It's all right, Mia,' Grandma said. 'I'm feeling a bit tired, so I'll have a nap now and you can tell me the rest later. I'll look forward to that.'

Grandma yawned and curled

up in her lovely warm bed, ready
to fall fast asleep.

Mia was wondering where
Clarissa the caterpillar could have
disappeared to, so she could tell
her grandma later.

'I need you to bring me some
bluebells,' Mia's mum said. 'You
can do that, can't you, Mia?'

'Easy-peasy,' said Mia. But
she was still thinking about the
story. *Where, oh, where would*

23

Archie find Clarissa?

Mia's mum looked at her.
'Are you sure you won't forget? I
know what you're like when you're
making up one of your stories –
you never have room in your head
to think about anything else! Try
to remember: I need you to get me
some bluebells.'

'Yes, yes, bluebells, I know,
Mum,' Mia said, as she hopped
down from the cushion. *Maybe*

Clarissa could be hiding in a big, spooky cave? Maybe she could be caught in a giant cobweb?

'Sleep well, Grandma,' Mia called as she scampered through the burrow. *Maybe Clarissa could have got stuck inside a rabbit hole?*

Mia raced through the tunnel that led out into Misty Wood. She jumped out of the little hole between the roots, opened her gauzy wings and floated up, up,

up into the sunshine.

'Clarissa the Giant Caterpillar! My best story ever!' the little Moss Mouse squeaked happily as she fluttered away.

CHAPTER TWO

Don't Forget . . .

Mia's wings glimmered and shone
as she flew through the bright
sunlight.

'I mustn't forget,' she muttered
to herself, 'Mum wants me to

bring her a . . . ooh! What's that?'

Some bright green leaves were hanging down from an oak tree nearby. They had huge holes in them, as if something had been eating them.

'Maybe a giant caterpillar ate those leaves!' Mia gasped. Her whiskers were twitching like mad. 'Maybe it was Clarissa!'

She swooped down to take a closer look.

The leaves did look just like

Clarissa had been chomping them

with her greedy munching jaws.

Mia landed on the tree branch

and skipped along it. Maybe she

29

would find a real life Clarissa up here! She searched everywhere, peering under the leaves, but she couldn't see a giant caterpillar.

I'm just like Archie the Ant! Mia thought to herself with a smile. *I'm hunting for Clarissa!*

Mia leaped off the branch and flitted between the trees. She had to get home to the burrow right away to tell Grandma the next part of her story. But . . . wait a minute!

30

The little Moss Mouse swooped
to a halt. Her mum had asked her
to fetch something. What was it?
She thought and thought but she
couldn't remember. Her head was
too full of thoughts about Clarissa
and Archie.

'Think, Mia, think!' she
squeaked.

I need you to bring me some b . . .

It was no good. Next, she tried
saying it out loud: 'I need you to

bring me some b . . .' But, try as she might, she couldn't remember what it was.

'It's something beginning with "B",' Mia said, scratching her furry head.

The little Moss Mouse looked at the trees and plants that were growing all around her. Then she started to smile. 'There must be lots of things in Misty Wood that begin with "B",' she said to herself.

'If I keep looking out for them, I'm bound to remember what it was that Mum wanted.'

She swirled her wings and whizzed off. Before long, she saw a fluffy brown fairy animal with floppy ears and beautiful golden wings hopping along the ground.

'A Bud Bunny!' Mia cried. 'That begins with a "B"!'

She watched the bunny leaping over the ferns. Why would

her mum want a Bud Bunny? It looked much too bouncy for the inside of Mia's burrow. And there weren't any buds there for it to open into flowers, which was the Bud Bunnies' special job.

'It can't be a Bud Bunny,' Mia
said, shaking her head.

Then she saw a big beech tree,
with wide branches stretching out
like huge arms.

'Oooh – I know!' Mia cried,
clapping her little paws together.
'A beechwood back scratcher!
Mum's always got an itchy back.'

But then Mia remembered
that her dad had made her mum
a beautiful back scratcher from a

piece of beechwood only the other day.

'I don't think Mum would want *another* back scratcher,' Mia said. 'After all, she's only got one back!'

She flew on through the wood until she saw some water, glinting in the sunlight.

'A babbling brook!' Mia squeaked. 'Mum would love one of those!'

She glided down and landed

softly on the bank of the brook.
The water was fresh and clear and
made a cheerful gurgling noise as
it rushed along.

Mia scampered across the
bank. She sat down and leaned
over to catch some of the water in
her paws.

'*Zzzz!*'

Mia jumped and nearly
tumbled into the brook. Something
was buzzing round her head!

'Beeeeee careful,' a buzzy voice said to her. 'You don't want to fall in.'

Then it stopped buzzing and landed on the bank in front of Mia. It was a fat, stripy bumble bee!

'Whatever are you doing?' the bee asked.

'I'm trying to catch the water,' Mia told him. 'My mum wants me to bring her a babbling brook.'

'Well, that'zzz very strange,'

said the bumble bee. 'Thizzz brook
flowzzz on for milezzz and milezzz.
It'zzz much too big to carry home.'

Mia sighed. 'Maybe I've got
it wrong. All I know for sure is

that she wants me to fetch her
something beginning with "B".'

The bumble bee frowned.
'Your mum muzzzt have meant
zzzomething elzzze,' he buzzed.

Mia looked at him and her
whiskers started to tremble with
excitement. 'I know! Maybe Mum
asked me to bring her a bumble bee!'

'Oh, I don't think so,' the bee
buzzed, backing away from Mia.

'We've got a lovely burrow,'

Mia said. 'You'd really like it.'

'But I need to be outzide,
making lotzz of lovely honey from
the flower nectar,' he replied with a
frown.

'Oh, yes.' Mia's whiskers
began to droop. 'Sorry, I didn't
mean to upset you. It's probably
not a bumble bee Mum wants
after all. I just wish I could
remember what it was.'

She sat down on the grass

and sniffed. She was feeling very fed up indeed. Her mum would be cross if she didn't remember!

The bumble bee rubbed his face with his front legs. 'Don't be sad,' he said. 'What'z your name?'

Mia looked up at him. 'Mia,' she said quietly.

'I'm Buzby,' he said. 'Buzby the bumble bee. Look, Mia, there are loadzz of thingzz in Misty Wood beginning with "B". I could

help you look for them.'

'Oh, thank you, Buzby!'
Mia fluttered into the air.

'And just in case it *iz* a
bumble bee she'z after,' Buzby
went on, 'I'll come back with you
to your burrow when we've finished
looking. But only for a vizit, mind
you. How about that?'

'That's so kind of you, Buzby,'
Mia said. She flapped her tiny
wings happily. 'Let's go!'

CHAPTER THREE

Searching Misty Wood!

Mia and Buzby fluttered through
the Heart of Misty Wood looking
for things beginning with 'B'. All
around them, sunbeams poked
through the leaves like long golden

44

fingers, making pretty patterns on the ground.

'Hey, Buzby!' Mia called. 'There's a birch tree. That begins with a "B".'

The bumble bee zoomed over to the tall birch tree that Mia was pointing to. Beautiful pictures of hearts and rainbows had been carved into its silver bark by the Bark Badgers.

'Too big,' Buzby buzzed. 'It'll

never fit inside your burrow.'

But Mia's whiskers were

twitching. 'What about the twigs?

We could make a bristly broomstick

with them! Maybe that's what Mum wants.'

Buzby looked doubtful. 'Hazzn't she got one already?' he asked.

Mia nodded. 'Yes, she has. She sweeps the burrow with it every day.'

'Then she won't be needing another one, will she? We'll have to look for something elze.'

They fluttered their wings and flew onwards until they came to a sunny clearing. A herd of

Dream Deer were bounding across the grass. Their legs were so long and they moved so gracefully that they looked as if they were dancing. Mia's whiskers twitched and twizzled. Her next idea was so much fun!

'Maybe Mum wants a ballet-dancing buffalo!' she squeaked. She was so excited she turned head-over-heels in the air.

Buzby looked very surprised.

'A buffalo? In Misty Wood? I've never seen one. Have you?'

'No, I suppose not,' Mia said, spinning the right way up again.

'Your imagination'z running away with you,' said Buzby. 'Let'z head back. Keep looking for thingz beginning with "B"!'

Mia followed him through the trees. Buzby was a very serious bumble bee. Maybe she could think of a story that would make

him laugh. Her whiskers twizzled
like mad.

'How about a boggley
boogaloo!' she squeaked.

Buzby stared at Mia. 'You just
made that up, didn't you?' he buzzed.

'Yes, I did!' Mia giggled.
Her whiskers twitched as more
ideas popped into her head. 'A
boogaloo's a bright yellow bug,
with big boggley eyes. And he
loves to . . . he loves to boogie!

I could tell you a story about him
if you like . . .'

But Buzby wasn't listening.
He'd seen something up ahead
and he was zooming towards it,
dodging between the tree trunks.

'Mia!' he called, 'come and zee!'

Mia's wings sparkled as she
hurried after him.

'What have you found?'

'Down there,' buzzed Buzby.

Mia looked down and saw a

bramble bush, stretching its thorny arms round the trunk of a tree. In between the thorns she could see . . .

'Blackberries!' she cried.

The two of them landed next to the bush. Sure enough, there were lots of juicy blackberries growing there, shiny and bright as jewels.

'Are these what your mum wanted?' asked Buzby.

Mia scratched her head with her tiny pink paw. 'I'm not sure,' she said. 'They do look delicious, though. Why don't we take some back to the burrow, just in case. But there are so many – how

shall we carry them?'

Buzby twirled his antennae. 'We need a bazket.'

Mia's whiskers twitched. 'Oh, Buzby – a basket begins with "B" too! Do you think that's what Mum wants?'

'I don't know,' said Buzby. 'But I know just where we can find one. Come on!'

He spun his little wings and leaped into the air, flying swiftly

towards the edge of Misty Wood. Mia followed him, until the trees began to thin out and she saw a long, leafy hedgerow.

There wasn't a basket to be seen. In fact, there wasn't anything at all beginning with 'B'!

'Why did we come out here, Buzby?' she called out.

'Follow me,' he buzzed, 'and you'll see!'

CHAPTER FOUR

Follow the Song!

'Come on,' Buzby called, pointing
with his front legs as he flew up to
the top of the hedge.

Mia raced after him. 'Wow!'
she gasped.

Hundreds of tiny, glittering dewdrops dangled from spiders' webs on the other side of the hedge. They looked like strings of diamonds.

'Those dewdrops are beautiful!' Mia cried. 'What a shame they don't begin with "B". Mum would love them!'

A white kitten with pale blue wings flew up to Mia. She was carrying a little basket made from

woven flower stems.

Mia's whiskers began to twirl.

'You're a Cobweb Kitten, aren't

you?' she said.

The kitten nodded.

'It's your job to decorate the spiders' webs,' Mia went on.

'That's right,' purred the kitten.

'You've done such a lovely job!' Mia said.

'Thank you.' The kitten smiled. 'Do help yourself to some of my dewdrops.'

'It's a bazket we need,' Buzby interrupted. 'We're looking for thingz beginning with "B".'

Mia nodded. 'My mum

asked me to bring her something
beginning with "B" and I've
forgotten what it is,' she explained
to the kitten. 'We've found some
lovely blackberries, but there are
too many for us to carry. If we had
a basket to put the blackberries in,
we'd have two things beginning
with "B"!'

'You can have my basket if
you like,' the friendly kitten said.
'It's very light, and I've got loads

more at home. I'll just hang these last few dewdrops.'

Mia watched as the kitten flew up and strung the bright droplets on the spider silk.

'Blackberries – how delicious,' the kitten purred as she handed the empty basket to Mia. 'I bet your mum will love them.'

'I think so too,' Mia said. 'I just hope they're what she asked me for. Thank you for your help!'

'Good luck,' called the kitten as Mia and Buzby headed back to the blackberry bush.

'I hope we *will* be lucky,' said Mia when they got back to the bush and began filling the basket.

'Shhh!' whispered Buzby. 'Lizzen!'

High up above their heads a bird was singing.

'Twee-twee! Twee-twee-twee!'

Mia looked up. A little bird

63

with bright blue
feathers the colour
of a summer sky was
circling high above them.

'A bluebird!' Mia cried. 'Maybe
that's what Mum wanted. Quick,
we've got to catch up with him!'

Gripping the basket tightly in her paws, Mia flew as fast as she could. But the little bird was too quick. His blue feathers flashed through the treetops as he darted away, singing, 'Twee-twee! Twee-twee-twee!'

'Follow the song!' cried Mia.

'Phew!' panted Buzby, spinning his wings so fast they disappeared in a blur. 'We'll never catch up with him!

Suddenly Buzby slowed down and sniffed the air. 'Ooh, Mia – what'z that lovely smell?'

A beautiful blue carpet of flowers stretched out down below them on the ground. Mia and Buzby were flying over Bluebell Glade. But Mia didn't have time

to think about lovely smells. She just wanted to catch up with the bluebird.

'Come on, Buzby! Don't slow down!' she called.

'I've never seen so many flowerz before,' panted Buzby.

'Twee-twee!' sang the bluebird,

far ahead of them. His voice was getting fainter.

'Quick!' cried Mia. 'We're going to lose him!'

'I wish we could go and pick some,' Buzby sighed, looking down at Bluebell Glade. 'They smell so nice.'

'Buzby, forget the flowers!' Mia cried. 'Come on!'

But, try as they might, Mia and Buzby couldn't keep up with

the bluebird. They whizzed along, swerving through the tree trunks until they came to Heather Hill. The bluebird had disappeared. They couldn't even hear his song anymore.

'Do you think we could stop for a minute,' puffed Buzby. 'I'm not used to flying so fast.'

They flopped down on a patch of grass in amongst the heather. Lots of little yellow flowers were

69

growing there, but Mia didn't
notice them. She felt really sad.
She was quite sure that her mum
had asked her for a bluebird, and
now they had lost him.

Mia tried to cheer herself up
by thinking about her story for
Grandma. Maybe in the next part
of the story, Archie the Ant could
come to Heather Hill to search
for his friend Clarissa. Maybe
he'd look for her through the dark,

shadowy places beneath the heather.

Mia peered between the twisty roots, imagining the little ant scurrying back and forth. There was no sign of Clarissa, but Mia noticed something else. Something blue.

'Buzby, what's that?' she said, pointing her paw at it.

'I'm not sure,' Buzby replied. 'I'll see if I can get it.'

Buzby flattened down his

wings and squeezed between the heather plants. He came back holding a bright blue feather in his antennae.

'It must have fallen when the bluebird flew over the hill,' he said.

'It's so soft.' Mia stroked the feather with her paw. 'Maybe Mum wanted a bluebird's *feather*,' she said, placing it in the basket. 'But we'd better keep on looking for other things that begin with "B".'

'I begin with "B"!' a voice
called out.

Mia was so surprised she
dropped the basket on her paw.
'Who said that?' she squeaked as
she rubbed her toe.

But there was no one there,

just the little yellow flowers growing in the grass. Mia stared at them. They were buttercups. And buttercups began with 'B'! It must have been a buttercup that spoke to her.

Mia picked some of the flowers and put them in the basket on top of the blackberries and the bluebird's feather.

'No!' came the voice again. 'Not them, *me*!'

The voice was calling from up above. Whoever it was sounded very cross.

'Who's that?' Mia squeaked in her bravest voice, and she half-covered her head with the little basket.

CHAPTER FIVE

Seeing Stars

'Please don't hide,' said the voice.

Mia peeped out from under

the basket. An insect with big purple

wings was floating in the air,

gazing down at her with huge eyes.

It was a beautiful butterfly.

'Hello!' the butterfly said, swishing her wings. 'I only shouted at you because I was so excited.

You see, I didn't always begin with a "B". In fact, up until last week, I began with a "C".'

Mia and Buzby stared at the butterfly, puzzled.

'What do you mean?' Mia asked.

'Well, I used to be a caterpillar. But *now* I'm a beautiful, brilliant, brightly-coloured butterfly – so I most definitely begin with "B"!'

Mia's heart gave a big jump

78

inside her. 'Your name isn't Clarissa, is it?' she asked.

The butterfly looked surprised. 'No. It's Buffy. Why do you ask?'

'Oh, never mind. It's just something to do with a story,' Mia said. 'It's very nice to meet you, Buffy. My name's Mia, and this is my friend, Buzby.'

'Nice to meet you too,' said Buffy.

Mia put her basket down and

began to explain how her mum had asked her for something beginning with 'B'. 'I just can't remember what it was though,' she finished with a sigh.

'It might be blackberriez,' Buzby said. 'Or buttercupz. Or possibly a bumble bee like me. Or perhapz a bazket, or a bluebird'z feather, or . . .'

'A butterfly!' Mia interrupted, her whiskers wiggling.

'Really?' Buffy looked pleased. 'Well, of course, I *am* one of the most beautiful butterflies in Misty Wood, so I wouldn't be at all surprised if it *is* me your mum wants. Why don't I come along with you?'

'Oh, yes, would you?' Mia cried. 'I know my mum would love your gorgeous wings.'

'You could help us look for some other thingz beginning with

"B", too,' Buzby said, and he got up from the grass and stretched out his little legs. 'Come on, let'z head back into Misty Wood!'

Buzby and Mia flew up to join Buffy as she fluttered off towards the trees. But Mia was so busy admiring Buffy's dazzling purple wings that she didn't look where she was going. All of a sudden – *oomph!* – she flew straight into a big tree trunk.

'Ouch!' squeaked Mia as she slid down the trunk and landed on the ground with a thud.

'Oh, no! Did you hurt yourself?' asked Buzby, landing softly beside her.

'Oooh,' said Mia, 'what lovely twinkly stars . . . pink ones and silver ones and . . .'

'Starz?' said Buzby, looking around. 'Where?'

'She's seeing stars because

she bumped her head,' Buffy

explained, fanning Mia with her

wings. 'Are you OK?'

'Yes, I think so,' Mia said, sitting up carefully. The stars had all disappeared now. 'It wasn't a bad bump. Thanks, Buffy.'

Something had fallen off the tree as Mia slid down it. She picked it up. It was a piece of bark.

'Maybe it was some bark Mum wanted!' she said. She turned the bark over and saw that it was covered in swirly lines and circles.

'What a beautiful pattern.

A Bark Badger must have made it,' Buffy said.

'Hey!' a gruff voice called.

Mia jumped in surprise. A stocky Bark Badger with a black-and-white stripy face and shiny silver wings was coming towards them. It must have been his tree she'd bumped into!

'I'm so s-s-sorry!' she stammered. 'I didn't mean to knock your bark off the tree. It was

86

an accident, I promise.'

The badger threw back his head and gave a hearty laugh.

'Don't worry, little Moss
Mouse,' he said in a booming
voice. 'You can keep that piece if
you like.'

Mia heaved a sigh of relief.
'Thanks!' she said. 'My friends
and I are collecting as many things
beginning with "B" as we can find
– for my mum.'

'I see.' The Bark Badger nodded
kindly. 'Can I help?' he asked.

'Wait a minute!' Buffy's purple

wings started to quiver. 'It might be a *Bark Badger* that your mum wants, Mia.'

Mia looked at the badger's big shoulders and his rough grey fur. It would be a tight squeeze fitting him into the burrow – but maybe Buffy was right.

'It *could* be a Bark Badger,' she said. 'But I'm not sure. Oh, I wish I could remember!'

The badger smiled. 'Well, why

don't I come along with you?'
he said. 'Just in case it *is* a Bark
Badger you need. My name's
Barney, by the way.'

'Thank you so much!' Mia
cried. 'Look at everything we've
collected!'

She held up her little pink paws
and began counting on her fingers.

'A bumble bee, a butterfly, a
Bark Badger, a bluebird's feather,
a piece of bark and a basket full

of buttercups and blackberries!'
She looked at her new friends
and smiled. 'I think we must have
everything beginning with "B" in
the whole of Misty Wood. Thank
you, everyone!'

The others smiled.

Buzby looked up at the sky.
'The sun'z going in,' he said. 'Iz it
tea time yet?'

'It must be,' said Mia. 'Come
on, let's head back to the burrow.

I bet Mum's made a cake.'

Barney picked up the basket
and the four friends flew off
through Misty Wood, with Mia
leading the way.

CHAPTER SIX

Two Happy Endings!

Mia scampered down the tunnel that led to her burrow, her new friends close behind her. 'Come on, everyone!' she called. 'Come and meet my mum!'

Mia's mum looked up in surprise as first Mia, then Buzby, then Buffy and finally Barney squeezed into the burrow.

'Well, I'm very glad I made such a big cake for tea,' she said. 'Mia, did you remember to bring me –'

But Mia didn't let her mum finish. 'I've brought loads of things!' she squeaked excitedly. 'Let's go over to Grandma's bed and I'll

show them to you!'

Mia's mum looked puzzled.

Mia scampered over, with
Buzby flying along at her side.

'I do hope we've got the thing
my mum wanted,' she whispered
to him.

'I'm sure you have,' Buzby
hummed, close to her ear. 'We've got
so many thingz beginning with "B".'

Grandma's little black eyes
nearly popped out of her head

when she saw all the visitors.

'Well, well, well!' she said.
'This is a surprise! Pull up a
cushion, why don't you? There's
plenty of them.'

Barney the Bark Badger
grinned as he sat down. He was
much too big to stand up in the
burrow. He kept bumping his
wings on the ceiling.

Mia looked at her mum.
'I know you wanted something

beginning with "B",' she started to explain, 'but I forgot what it was. So I brought you everything beginning with "B" that I could find. There's a bumble bee . . .'

Buzby stood up and gave a little bow. 'Buzby, at your service, Ma'am,' he said.

'Lovely to meet you, Buzby,' Mia's mum said. 'But I'm afraid it wasn't a bumble bee I wanted.'

'Well, how about a butterfly?'

asked Mia. 'This is Buffy.'

Buffy gave a twirl so that everyone could see her pretty lilac wings.

Mia's mum shook her head. 'You look lovely, Buffy. But it wasn't a butterfly I was after.'

'Oh, dear.' Mia was beginning to feel worried. 'Was it a Bark Badger, Mum? Because I brought Barney just in case.'

Barney raised a front paw.

TWO HAPPY ENDINGS!

'How do you do,' he said grandly.
'I'm very happy to help out.'

'That's very good of you,'
Mia's mum said. 'But I'm afraid I
don't need a Bark Badger either.'

Mia bit her lip. This wasn't
going well at all. She picked up the
basket.

'How about this lovely basket?'

Mia's mum shook her head.

Mia's whiskers drooped down
below her mouth.

'Show her what'z inside the bazket!' Buzby buzzed quietly. 'There are still lotz of thingz beginning with "B".'

'OK,' Mia whispered. She pulled out the bluebird's feather and showed it to her mum. 'Was it this?'

'No, Mia,' her mum replied. 'But that's a nice feather. I can weave it into the quilt I'm making for the babies' cot.'

101

'What about this?' Mia held up the piece of bark.

'Bark's always useful,' Mia's mum said. 'And I love the pattern. But I didn't ask for a piece of bark. What I wanted was –'

'These?' Mia squeaked, tipping up the basket so that all the juicy blackberries spilled out.

'No, not blackberries, though they'll be lovely to have with our tea,' Mia's mum said.

There was just one thing left.

'Buttercups!' cried Mia,
holding up the bunch of bright
yellow flowers. 'Please tell me
that's what you wanted!'

Mia's mum sighed. 'No, Mia. I'm sorry, but it wasn't buttercups I asked you to bring either.'

Mia sat back on her hind legs and sighed. 'What in Misty Wood could it be? I thought I'd collected *everything* beginning with "B".'

'Bluebells,' Mia's mum said gently. 'I asked for some bluebells.'

'Some *bluebells*?' Mia gasped.

'Oh, no!' groaned Buzby. He hid his face in his front legs. 'Mia

– we flew over hundredz of them in Bluebell Glade . . .'

Mia nodded. 'Yes, when we were chasing the bluebird. We didn't stop to think. What do you want the bluebells for, Mum?'

'To put on the cushion you made for Grandma,' Mia's mum said. 'All it needs are some bluebell decorations to make it quite perfect.'

'Grandma, I'm so sorry!' Mia burst into tears. 'I've been a silly

Moss Mouse. Your cushion would have looked so pretty with some bluebells to finish it off!'

Grandma's nose wrinkled in a smile.

'Don't cry, Mia,' she said. 'I'm not upset that you forgot about the bluebells. Because you *did* bring some buttercups – and they're my favourite flowers in the world!'

'Really?' Mia sniffed.

'Really and truly,' her

grandma replied. 'They're so very bright and cheerful, they make me think of sunshine. I'd much rather have buttercups than bluebells on my cushion.'

Mia wiped her eyes and fixed some of the buttercups on to Grandma's moss cushion. They looked beautiful, and everybody clapped and cheered.

'Well done,' said Mia's mum. 'You might have forgotten the

bluebells, Mia, but you've made Grandma very happy with those buttercups. Now, shall I go and fetch the tea?'

Buzby, Buffy and Barney all said they would help.

'I'll come too!' Mia said.

Grandma shook her head. 'Stay here with me, Mia,' she said. 'I want to hear the rest of your story. Sit on the buttercup cushion beside me and tell me more about

Clarissa the Caterpillar.'

Mia jumped on to the cushion. 'D'you remember, Grandma, how Clarissa disappeared, and her friend Archie the Ant couldn't find her?' she asked.

Grandma nodded.

'Well . . .' Mia's whiskers wiggled. She told Grandma how Archie had searched everywhere. He'd climbed up a big tall tree – how scary that was! And he'd

hunted all through the roots of the heather plants on Heather Hill, but Clarissa was nowhere to be seen.

'So where was she?' Grandma asked.

Mia's whiskers were twizzling so much. She knew Grandma would love the end of the story.

'There was one place Archie hadn't looked – Moonshine Pond. He trudged all the way there through Misty Wood. His legs were aching

so much he could hardly walk.'

'Poor Archie,' said Grandma.
'I feel quite sorry for him.'

'When he got to the pond
there was no sign of Clarissa.'
Mia went on. 'There was only a
beautiful butterfly admiring her
reflection in the water. Archie
started to cry. "I miss my friend
Clarissa!" he said. The butterfly
flew over and sat beside him on
the grass. "Don't be sad," she said.

"It's me. *I'm* Clarissa.'"

'Well, I never!' Grandma said.

'Archie didn't believe her,'
continued Mia. 'But Clarissa
explained that all caterpillars eat
lots and lots and get bigger and
bigger and then they disappear
for a while until they turn into
butterflies. She thanked Archie for
bringing her all those lovely snacks
to eat when she was a caterpillar.

"'You've helped me become

the most beautiful butterfly in Misty Wood," she said. "I'll be your best friend for ever and ever." Archie was so happy he forgot how tired he was and he danced all the way round Moonshine Pond. The End!'

'Oh, Mia!' said Grandma with a big smile. 'I love a happy ending.'

'Did I hear someone say "snacks"?' called Mia's mum. She trotted up to Grandma's bed, carrying the piece of bark.

On top of it was a cake made from crunchy hazelnuts.

Buzby and Buffy followed her, carrying acorns filled with blackberry juice. Mia's dad came too, with some plump barleycorns he'd found while he was out collecting moss.

And last of all came Barney, carrying Mia's baby brothers and sisters in the basket so they could join in the tea party.

TWO HAPPY ENDINGS!

Everybody sat down around Grandma and began eating and drinking. Mia snuggled up with Grandma in her mossy bed, and nibbled some cake.

'Look at all the things I found!' she said, when she'd finished her cake. 'Bumble bee, blackberries, basket, butterfly . . .'

'I can think of something else beginning with "B",' Grandma whispered, when Mia got to the

end of the list.

'What?' asked Mia, looking around. She saw the grains of barley that her dad had brought.

'Is it "barleycorns", Grandma?'

'They're tasty, but no, that's not what I meant,' Grandma said.

Then Mia saw her four brothers and sisters sipping their blackberry juice. 'Do you mean "babies", Grandma?'

Grandma laughed. 'That's a

good guess! But no. You've brought so many wonderful things today, Mia – especially those beautiful buttercups. But the most special thing of all is that I feel *better*. You told me such a lovely story and made me such a beautiful cushion that I forgot all about my cold. It's quite gone away! You've made me feel *better*, and that's the *best* thing of all.'

Mia looked at Grandma's

smiling face. Then she looked at her mum, who was showing Buzby and Buffy and Barney how to make a moss cushion. They weren't very good at it and everybody was laughing and giggling as they rolled the moss around. Then she looked at her dad, who was tickling the babies with the bluebird's feather and making them laugh.

Everybody was so happy.

Perhaps I'm not so silly after all, Mia thought, and she cuddled up next to Grandma and helped herself to another piece of her mum's delicious cake.

Turn the page for lots of fun Misty Wood activities!

Mia's mum asked her to find some bluebells. Can you help Mia follow the right path?

Mia spent the day in Misty Wood
trying to find things beginning with B.
She founds lots and lots of things!

Why not go on a treasure hunt in
your garden, or in the park with your
parent or guardian.

Write down all the things
you find in the space below.

Things beginning with 'a'

....

....

....

Things beginning with 'b'

....

....

....

Things beginning with 'c'

....

....

....

Spot the difference

The picture on the opposite page is slightly different to this one.
Can you circle all the differences?

Moss Mice, like Mia, love making and decorating soft, beautiful moss cushions for the fairy animals to sleep on.

Use the outline on the next page to design and decorate your very own moss cushion!

Misty Wood Word search

Use the words below to create your own word search! Write all the words in the boxes and fill the other spaces with lots of different letters. Then show it to a friend and see if they can solve it!

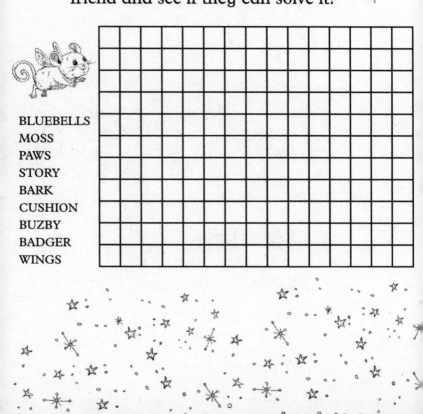

BLUEBELLS
MOSS
PAWS
STORY
BARK
CUSHION
BUZBY
BADGER
WINGS

Fairy Animals
of Misty Wood

Meet all the fairy animal friends!

Lily Small

Chloe the Kitten

Fairy Animals
of Misty Wood

Bella the Bunny

Fairy Animals
of Misty Wood

Paddy the Puppy

Fairy Animals
of Misty Wood

Mia the Mouse

Fairy Animals
of Misty Wood

Look out for Hailey the Hedgehog
and lots more coming soon . . .

Lily Small

Hailey the Hedgehog

Fairy Animals
of Misty Wood